大象的秘密花園

the elephant's secret garden

林帥Shine Lin 著

Self introduction

I'm shine, I'm 7 year old. I like read book and play games. And I like to ride a bike. I hope to have more friends. I enjoy playing and learning new things.

I'll introduce you this book. The book is fun. I hope you like it.

Shine Lin
林郎

這是一本

由小學二年級的帥帥

自己編的故事

爸爸引導故事的完整

藉由AI 繪圖軟體

讓孩子創意落地

讓孩子想像力飛翔

作者簡歷：林帥

Podcast：帥帥講故事/ 主講

學歷：小學二年級

一個用AI 讓孩子創意落地的故事

小帥是我第一個孩子，而我是一個科技創業家老爸，除了陪小帥上山下海，更不忘用擅長的科技，讓孩子的想像力盡情飛翔。

小帥從2歲開始，就引導他開始哼哼丫丫的說著或許只有他自己聽得懂的故事，我也把這個講故事的過程，錄製成時下最夯的Podcast 節目「帥帥說故事」，上架後，帥帥的童言童語竟也吸引了不少小小粉絲，讓孩子樂不可支。每每夜深人靜，聽著過去孩子稚嫩的聲音，我總忍不住沉浸於當時與孩子共錄Podcast的幸福回憶。

隨著Open AI與ChatGTP的熱烈討論，身為科技老爸的我，想的不是商業應用，而是如何讓這套神奇的工具，讓帥帥無限的想像力與故事力繼續延伸。也因此，我與帥帥共同創作了第一本透過AI輔助，以孩子為創作核心的繪本。

有時候在想，為什麼小朋友的繪本都是大人畫的、寫的；擁有無限想像力的孩子難道不能創作繪本嗎？孩子創作的繪本，是不是更能與同樣是孩子的讀者產生共鳴？有了AI的幫助，帥帥可以講述自己編的故事，爸爸引導他讓故事更完整，帥帥自己對著AI繪圖軟體訴說著對於故事無限的想像，AI快速的回應著帥帥對於圖像的指令，這一系列的過程，都讓帥帥歡欣不已。就在這樣一個引導、聆聽、訴說的過程中，我們完成了第一本AI 幫助帥帥一起創作的孩童繪本。

這本書的故事與圖案或許不是最精美、最有特色的，但卻是每個小孩獨一無二、無可取代的創意表現，更是親子互動與科技輔助的最佳代表。這整個過程的美好與孩子看到自己創作時的成就感，只有親身體會才能知道。

現在，帥爸我誠摯地邀請你，一起加入這個用AI讓孩子創意落地，讓想像力飛翔的過程，也希望你跟你的孩子喜歡這本書。

最後，澄清一下家長看完本書可能產生的兩個誤會：

圖案是AI產生的（AIGC），孩子只是指導AI畫出想要的構圖，我從旁給AI下指令。

故事內容是取材自王爾德的一篇文章，孩子聽後重新改編講述出來，為了出版考量，文字有經過大人做了一些加工。

林政宏（帥爸）
2023/02/20

很久很久以前， 在一所小學的旁邊， 有一座大花園，
每天放學以後， 小朋友們都喜歡到花園裡玩耍。

A long long time ago, next to a primary school, there was a large garden where the children loved to play after school every day.

但是，有一天，花園的主人回來了，
花園的主人，是一隻大象，長得又高又壯，
他有長長的鼻子，和粗粗的象腿。

One day, however, the owner of the garden returned, and the owner of the garden was an elephant, tall and strong, with a long trunk and thick legs.

大象不喜歡小朋友到他的花園裡玩，
所以他把全部小朋友，都趕走了。

The elephant didn't like the children playing in his garden, so he chased all of them away.

從那天以後， 美麗的春天， 好像把這個花園給忘記了。

After that day, it was as if the beautiful spring had forgotten about the garden.

為什麼呢？
因為，
春天的時候，花園外面到處都開滿了小花，
還有好多可愛的小鳥在唱歌。

Why?
Because during the spring, there were small flowers blooming
everywhere outside of the garden,
and many lovely birds singing.

可是， 花園裡面還在下雪哦，
天氣好冷好冷， 北風呼～ 呼的， 一直在吹。

It's still snowing in the garden, and the weather is very cold.
The north wind is howling and blowing constantly.

大象覺得很奇怪， 明明春天應該要到了，
為什麼花園裡的雪， 還下得這麼大呢？

The elephant feels very strange. Spring should be coming, but why is it
still snowing so heavily in the garden?

原來， 因為花園裡的小朋友， 被大象趕走， 不見了，
所以， 美麗的小花忘記開了， 小鳥也不想唱歌了。
大象覺得這個冬天非常漫長， 好像永遠都不會過去。

Actually, it was because the children in the garden were driven away by the elephant and disappeared. Therefore, the beautiful flowers forgot to bloom, and the birds did not want to sing.
The elephant feels that this winter is very long, as if it will never end.

有一天早上， 大象懶洋洋的躺在床上， 不想起床，
突然， 窗戶外面傳來美妙的音樂。

One morning, the elephant was lying lazily in bed and didn't want to get up.
But just then, a beautiful melody drifted in through the open window.

這是他聽過， 在世界上最好聽的音樂。

Never before had the elephant heard such enchanting music in the world.

音樂一直在唱，
過了不久，
大雪停下來了，
北風呢， 也不再呼～ 呼的吹了。

The music kept playing, and soon, the heavy snow stopped falling.
The north wind also stopped howling.

嗯～ 好香啊，
一陣花的香味從窗戶飄進來，
大象趕緊跳下床看。

"Mmm, it smells wonderful!"
A sweet floral fragrance wafted in through the window,
and the elephant quickly jumped out of bed to investigate.

大象看到什麼了呢？ 大象看到一幅很美妙的畫面。

What did the elephant see? The elephant saw a breathtakingly beautiful scene.

一群小朋友， 開心的在樹上，
跳啊笑啊， 發出像鈴鐺一樣的聲音。

A group of children joyfully jumping and laughing on a tree,
creating sounds like bells.

之前，大象不讓小朋友進來花園玩，把花園的大門關起來了。

Before that, the elephant wouldn't let the children play in the garden and closed the gate.

調皮的小朋友們， 就想了別的辦法，
他們從牆壁旁邊的小洞， 鑽進花園。

The mischievous children came up with another idea and crawled into the garden through a small hole next to the wall.

小朋友們回到花園了，
樹爺爺很高興，他已經好久，
沒有聽到小朋友的笑聲了。

The children had returned to the garden, and the tree grandpa was delighted.
It had been a long time since he last heard the children's laughter.

天上的小鳥，飛來飛去，嘰嘰喳喳的，
花園裡的薔薇也開得好漂亮啊！

The little birds in the sky flit about, chirping and chattering away,
while the roses in the garden are blooming so beautifully!

咦ˊ， 大ㄉㄚˋ象ㄒㄧㄤˋ往ㄨㄤˇ旁ㄆㄤˊ邊ㄅㄧㄢ一ㄧ看ㄎㄢˋ，
發ㄈㄚ現ㄒㄧㄢˋ花ㄏㄨㄚ園ㄩㄢˊ的ㄉㄜ角ㄐㄧㄠˇ落ㄌㄨㄛˋ邊ㄅㄧㄢ， 怎ㄗㄣˇ麼ㄇㄜ還ㄏㄞˊ像ㄒㄧㄤˋ冬ㄉㄨㄥ天ㄊㄧㄢ一ㄧ樣ㄧㄤˋ，
在ㄗㄞˋ下ㄒㄧㄚˋ雪ㄒㄩㄝˇ咧ㄌㄧㄝ！

Oh, when the elephant looked to the side, he found that the corner of the garden seemed to be snowing like in winter!

在角落邊， 有一個小男孩，
他很努力的爬樹，
但是， 他的個子太小了，
怎麼樣都爬不上去。

In the corner, a little boy was trying his best to
climb a tree, but he was just too small to reach
the top.

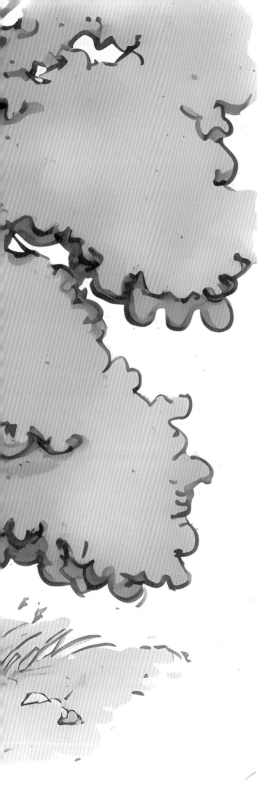

所以，北風用他的力氣，
用力的，吹啊吹，
想幫助小男孩爬到樹上。

So, the North wind used its strength and
blew with all its might, trying to help the
little boy climb up the tree.

樹ㄕㄨ爺ㄧㄝ爺ㄧㄝ也ㄧㄝ把ㄅㄚ腰ㄧㄠ彎ㄨㄢ下ㄒㄧㄚ來ㄌㄞ，
讓ㄖㄤ小ㄒㄧㄠ男ㄋㄢ孩ㄏㄞ離ㄌㄧ他ㄊㄚ更ㄍㄥ近ㄐㄧㄣ一ㄧ點ㄉㄧㄢ。

The tree grandpa also bent down to bring
the little boy closer to him.

大象看到北風和樹爺爺，
都在幫助小男孩，
心裡很感動。

The elephant was deeply moved upon
seeing both the north wind and tree
grandpa lending a helping hand to the
little boy.

大象覺得自己不讓小朋友到花園來玩，
有點小氣。

The elephant felt a twinge of selfishness for not allowing the children to come and play in the garden.

所以， 他決定要推倒花園的圍牆，
歡迎所有的小朋友， 都來花園一起玩。

So, he decided to knock down the garden fence and welcome all the children to come and play together in the garden.

大象悄悄的，
走到花園門口，
準備打開厚重的大門。

The elephant quietly walked towards the gate, preparing to open the thick and heavy door.

可ㄎㄜˇ是ㄕˋ，
小ㄒㄧㄠˇ朋ㄆㄥˊ友ㄧㄡˇ看ㄎㄢˋ到ㄉㄠˋ大ㄉㄚˋ象ㄒㄧㄤˋ走ㄗㄡˇ過ㄍㄨㄛˋ來ㄌㄞˊ，
都ㄉㄡ紛ㄈㄣ紛ㄈㄣ嚇ㄒㄧㄚˋ跑ㄆㄠˇ了ㄌㄜ˙⋯⋯

However, when the children saw the elephant
approaching, they all fled in fear.

突然之間，花園又回到之前冬天的模樣，
北風呼～呼的吹個不停，
小鳥全部都飛走了，
花朵也枯萎了。

Suddenly, the garden had reverted to its winter appearance.
The strong north wind was howling ceaselessly, and all the birds had
flown away.
The flowers had withered.

不ㄅㄨˋ過ㄍㄨㄛˋ，
有ㄧㄡˇ一ㄧ個ㄍㄜˋ小ㄒㄧㄠˇ朋ㄆㄥˊ友ㄧㄡˇ沒ㄇㄟˊ有ㄧㄡˇ跑ㄆㄠˇ掉ㄉㄧㄠˋ，
就ㄐㄧㄡˋ是ㄕˋ角ㄐㄧㄠˇ落ㄌㄨㄛˋ邊ㄅㄧㄢ那ㄋㄚˋ個ㄍㄜˋ小ㄒㄧㄠˇ男ㄋㄢˊ孩ㄏㄞˊ。

However, there was one child who didn't run away,
the little boy in the corner.

小男孩想爬到樹上， 但是他怎麼爬都上不去，

The little boy wanted to climb the tree, but no matter how hard he tried, he couldn't manage to climb up.

他的眼睛溼溼的， 看起來很傷心。

His eyes were moist, and he looked very sad.

大象走到小男孩身邊，
把他抱了起來， 很輕鬆的就放到樹上。

The elephant walked up to the little boy, picked him up with ease, and placed him on the tree.

哇～一下子，
樹馬上就開花了，
小鳥也飛過來唱歌。

Wow, all of a sudden,
the tree bloomed,
and little birds flew over to sing.

小男孩高興極了，抱住大象的脖子，
啵～ 親了大象一下。

The little boy was extremely happy and hugged the
elephant's neck, giving him a big kiss.

大象也笑得好開心啊， 這小男孩就是
大象的第一個朋友。

The elephant also laughed happily. This little boy was the
elephant's first friend.

從此以後， 大象的花園，
變成熱鬧的遊樂場，
整天嘻嘻哈哈，
都是小朋友的笑聲，
而且啊， 花園裡一年四季， 都開著美麗的花。

Since then, the elephant's garden has turned into a bustling playground,
filled with the laughter of children playing and having fun all day long.
Moreover, beautiful flowers bloom in the garden throughout the year.

大象的秘密花園
The elephant's secret garden

作　　者　林帥 Shine Lin
編　　輯　林政宏
圖　　片　由Midjourney生成／林帥製作
出　　版　雲書苑教育科技有限公司
　　　　　臺北市北投區明德路79號2樓
　　　　　網址：www.ABC123.im
　　　　　信箱：key@ppvs.org
　　　　　電話：02-28230833
設計編印　白象文化事業有限公司
　　　　　專案主編：陳婷婷　經紀人：張輝潭
經銷代理　白象文化事業有限公司
　　　　　412台中市大里區科技路1號8樓之2（台中軟體園區）
　　　　　出版專線：（04）2496-5995　　傳眞：（04）2496-9901
　　　　　401台中市東區和平街228巷44號（經銷部）
　　　　　購書專線：（04）2220-8589　　傳眞：（04）2220-8505
印　　刷　基盛印刷工場
初版一刷　2023年7月
定　　價　250元

國家圖書館出版品預行編目資料

大象的秘密花園 The elephant's secret garden
／林帥(Shine Lin) 圖/文. --初版.--臺北市：
雲書苑教育科技有限公司，2023.7
　　面；21X29.7公分
國語注音,中英對照
ISBN 978-626-97230-0-3（精裝）

863.599　　　　　　　　　　112003354